The Dragon Island

Diana Molly

Introduction

When Monica goes to gather flowers in the forest, she doesn't have any idea that her most adventurous day is about to begin. Her day starts with finding a strange egg, which is as tall as she is!

As she goes through different islands, she realizes that one is stranger than the other and being a kind and brave girl, Monica solves all the problems together with her precious friend.

Will Monica be able to help her friend find her island at last? Or will they get into breathtaking adventures that never stop?

Monica teaches her friend determination and courage, which helps them a lot during their adventures..

Chapter 1. The Strange Egg

Singing and waving her straw-woven basket from side to side, a ten year-old girl was walking in the beautiful green forest and gathering flowers. Monica liked to gather flowers, especially in spring, when the forests were full of them in their little magical island Prettyland. She liked to make hair accessories from the colorful flowers and to put them in her long blond hair. She made hair accessories for her friends, too, who also liked to go to the forest with her to pick flowers.

But on that day she was alone: Nancy was busy helping her mother bake cookies, Julia was visiting her grandma and Lily was busy doing her homework. Monica had already finished her homework and had nothing else to do, so she had gone to the forest alone.

Her basket was almost full of different flowers: she had made sure to pick up different ones, as the hair accessories would be prettier that way. Suddenly she saw a big grey thing in front of her and stopped.

"What's this?" She said aloud. The thing looked like an egg, except that it was huge – almost her height. It could be a rock, too, but it was so perfectly smooth, that she didn't think it could be a rock.

After looking at it for a few seconds, Monica decided to roll it down the path into her village. Her mother and father would certainly know what it was. She put her basket on the ground and started to roll it. The egg was heavy, but she managed to roll it a bit.

Suddenly the egg hit a nearby big rock and stopped. Monica heard a cracking sound and saw that a narrow gap had appeared on the egg.

"Oh, no!" She exclaimed. "How will I take this egg to my village now?!"

In front of her eyes the gap got wider and wider, until two purple big feet appeared out of it and the egg started to run into the depth of the forest.

"The egg is running! The egg is running!" Monica started shouting, running after the egg. While running, two purple small arms and hands also appeared out of it. Then a small purple head of an animal appeared. Monica couldn't tell what kind of animal it was, because she was running after it and couldn't see its face.

The entire shell of the egg burst open and fell to the sides, and Monica saw that she was running after a purple dragon, which was a bit taller than her.

"Oh, that's a dragon!" She exclaimed. The dragon heard her voice and stopped running. It turned back to look at her. It was a very pretty dragon, with pink wings and bluish-purple body. The dragon looked at Monica with surprised eyes and came one step forward.

"Hello," Monica said, coming one step forward, too. "My name is Monica."

The dragon smiled. "Hello Monica. I don't know what my name is. And I don't know why I'm here. I want to go to the island where my parents live."

"You still don't have a name because you just came out of your egg," Monica said, "Let's think a name for you."

"Egg-born?" The dragon suggested.

"Maybe, but it doesn't sound beautiful," Monica said, shaking her head. "Maybe Prettywing?"

"I don't know…" the dragon shrugged. "What about Fireball?"

"But you can't make fire yet," Monica said. She thought for a moment, and then her face brightened. "Violet! We'll name you Violet! Because of your color!"

The dragon became very joyful, nodding in agreement. She liked her name very much.

"Thank you Monica for the beautiful name," she said. "Now please tell me how to go home."

"But where is your home?" Monica asked.

"On the Dragon Island. It's called Dragonland," Violet said. "When I was in the egg, a magical wind blew and took me away from there. I could hear everything while I was in my egg. But how can I get there?"

"I have never heard of Dragonland," Monica said. "I only know about Prettyland. Of course I know that there are many islands besides Prettyland, but I don't know what they are or how to get there."

"Will you help me find my island, Monica?" Violet asked, looking at her hopefully.

"I will come with you and try to find your parents," Monica said with determination. "Only I don't know where to go."

"We can swim the ocean and get to the other island," Violet suggested happily.

"Oh, no, we can't swim the ocean – it's too large," Monica said. "But why do you want to swim if you can fly? You are a dragon and you have wings!"

"Really! And why hadn't I thought about it?!" Violet exclaimed. "And how are you going to fly? You're not a dragon, after all."

"I hope I'm not too heavy," Monica said, smiling. "I can sit on your back, and we'll fly together. But if I'm too heavy for you, then we can think of something else."

"That's a great idea! Let's give it a try," Violet said, kneeling. Monica mounted the dragon easily.

"You're as light as a feather," Violet said. "Now let's try flying." With this she opened her wings and started moving them up and down. After a few seconds the dragon flew up into the air, with Monica on her back, hugging her tightly.

Chapter 2. A New Island

The scenery below was breathtaking. They were flying above treetops, almost touching them and enjoying the small waterfalls and sparkling rivers below.

"Violet, it's so beautiful!" Monica said. "I have never flown in my life."

"Neither have I," Violet said. "And I like it!"

Soon the forest ended and the ocean opened in front of them in all its blue beauty.

"Wow, Violet! Look, that's the ocean!"

"It's magnificent! Hold on tightly, Monica, be careful not to fall off!" Violet said and flew faster. She descended a bit and flew closely to the ocean, so that their feet splashed into the water, making them giggle with joy.

The sun was shining brightly and the sky was

blue. Soon Monica noticed land.

"I can see land, Violet! Let's go and see what it is. Maybe it's Dragonland!"

Violet became very excited. She flew as fast as she could until they reached solid ground and got down. Monica dismounted and looked around. It looked like a pretty green island, but it seemed to be empty.

"Violet, I don't see any dragons here," Monica said. Violet was confused.

"Then where is Dragonland?!" She asked.

"We have to find out," Monica said with determination. "Let's walk."

They started walking through the green grass, thick trees and colorful flowers, which seemed to be sparkling under the bright sun in different colors. As they walked, they started noticing different small animals that were living there: squirrels, rabbits, hamsters and mice.

"Welcome to Littleland, our island," one of the squirrels said, coming closer. "Who are you?"

"I am Monica, and this is my friend Violet. We want to go to Dragonland, but we don't know the way. Do you know where it is?"

"I'm sorry, but I have never heard of Dragonland," the squirrel said. "But you can stay here – this is a wonderful island, and everyone will welcome you."

Violet looked at Monica, looking very worried. "Thank you very much, but I want to go to my parents," she said politely. "We'll try to find my island."

The squirrel waved and went away.

"What shall we do now, Monica?" Violet said sadly. "What if my island doesn't exist?"

"Don't worry, Violet, we will find your island and your parents, I'm sure of it!" Monica said.

They continued walking. Something caught Monica's eyes: a little mouse was stuck under a rock and couldn't walk, while his family was walking and was ahead of him. The mice didn't seem to have noticed that the smallest mouse was missing.

"Help, help," the mouse was squeaking.

"Oh, look, Violet, this little mouse can't get out!" Monica said and lifted the rock. The little mouse smiled and ran as fast as he could. A few moments later he returned with his father.

"Are you the kind girl who rescued my kid?" The father asked Violet.

"No, I'm a dragon, but my friend Monica is," Violet said happily.

"Thank you, Monica," the father said. "How can I be grateful?"

"There's a question I wanted to ask, Mr. Mouse," Monica said. "We are looking for Dragonland. Do you know where it is?"

"I don't know exactly where it is, but I know that it exists," the father mouse said. "If you head to the east, you will go in the right direction."

"All right, thank you very much, we'll head east now," Violet said, getting excited again.

"You are welcome," the father mouse said, waved and went away.

"Come on, Monica," Violet said. "Let's fly! We will reach my parents soon!"

Monica mounted and they flew off. The island looked very beautiful from above, but soon it also disappeared and they were flying above the ocean again.

"I wonder where the next island will be," Monica said, looking around, while Violet flapped her wings and flew. The warm breeze was playing in Monica's beautiful blond hair, making it look like golden threads under the sunshine.

"I can see something a bit far away," Violet suddenly said, sounding excited. "I think it's an island! I hope it's Dragonland!"

Monica looked attentively and also saw it. "We're heading in the right direction!" she screamed.

The land was quickly drawing closer. Soon they

were flying above it. There was a blue narrow river going through it, turning abruptly to the side and floating into the ocean. There weren't any mountains or forests, but the entire island was covered with flowers.

Chapter 3. Where Is the Water?

"Oh, Violet! Look down!" Monica said. "This island is entirely made of flowers!"

"Let's get down and see what flowers they are," Violet suggested.

"What a wonderful idea!" Monica exclaimed. "I love flowers! And I like to make beautiful hair accessories from them. These are so colorful! I have never seen such flowers in our forests."

They got down and started walking through the flowers. Monica was jumping through the flowers joyfully, while Violet was sniffing them.

Suddenly Monica heard Violet scream: "Help! Help me, Monica!"

She turned abruptly to see what had happened. At first she didn't understand, but then she saw that one of Violet's hands was inside the petals of one red flower.

"What's happening, Violet?" She asked, running closer.

"This flower! It's biting me!" Violet shrieked. "It wants to eat me."

"To eat you?" Monica asked, with wide eyes. "What are you talking about? How can flowers eat a dragon?"

She walked closer to have a better look. She was sure Violet was joking, but at that moment something caught her leg.

"Ouch!" She screamed and looked down. A big flower was biting her leg with its petals. Monica looked at Violet, looking rather surprised. They looked around and saw that the other flowers were slowly moving towards them, their petals shivering in the mild breeze.

"Monica, we have to go away! The flowers want to eat us!" Violet was shrieking.

Monica didn't say anything. She was examining the leaves and stems of the flowers. They were dried up and wilted.

"Violet, look, these flowers seem thirsty!" Monica said. "Look at their leaves and stems. They seem to be thirsty, don't you think so?"

"So what that they are thirsty, Monica?" Violet said, trying to shake her hand free from the malicious flower. "I don't want them to drink me!"

"While we were flying up in the sky above this island, I noticed that the stream wasn't flowing through the entire island," Monica said. "And I wonder why. I think if the stream flew through the island, then the flowers wouldn't be thirsty."

"And what do you suggest us to do?"

"Let's at first break free, and then fly to the stream and see why it doesn't flow through this valley."

"But how can we break free, Monica? This flower is biting my hand, and the others are moving closer to catch my feet probably."

"But you still have your wings, Violet!" Monica said. "I can't walk, but you can fly! Try to fly and when you get free, pick me up, too."

The idea sounded good. Violet concentrated on flipping her wings, and using all her strength she managed to fly. The flower that was biting her hand had to let her go, but looked very angry.

"Yes, Violet! You managed it!" Monica shouted. "Now come and pick me up, because this nasty flower is really biting my leg!"

Violet flew closer to Monica and held her. Together they flew upwards, leaving the flowers angry and disappointed.

"Your idea was a great one," Violet said. "Now where shall we go?"

"To the stream we earlier saw on this island," Monica said. "I want to know why it isn't flowing through the valley."

They didn't have to fly long, as the stream was near. They landed right where the narrow river was changing direction and saw that a big rock was blocking the way of the stream to the valley.

"See, Violet?" Monica exclaimed, pointing to the rock. "This is the reason the flowers of the valley are so thirsty and wilted."

"But what can we do, Monica?" Violet asked, looking at the big rock.

"I think we must remove this rock," Monica said after thinking for a while. "Maybe then the stream will flow to the valley as well."

"Let's try, but it's very heavy," Violet said, trying to move the heavy rock. It didn't even move an inch.

"Look, Violet, it's too heavy for you alone," Monica said. "What if I push it and you hold onto it tightly and try to fly? Together we are stronger."

"Sounds easy," Violet said. "Let's give it a try."

Monica stepped on the side of the rock, careful not to fall into the stream, and started to push the rock with all her might. Violet flew above the rock, clutching it with her two hands as tightly as possible.

"Violet, try to take the rock away!" Monica called, pushing the rock as hard as she could.

Violet didn't say anything. She was concentrating. Finally the rock moved a little bit to the side.

"Some more!" Monica called. Violet tried harder, and finally the rock was out of the way. The stream changed direction and started to flow towards the valley where the flowers grew.

"Monica, we did a good job!" Violet exclaimed. "Now the flowers will be fresh and nice again."

Chapter 4. Are These Clouds or...?

Monica and Violet were flying in the sky. They were looking down at the valley where the flowers were slowly moving their heads in the breeze, as if waving them goodbye. The stream was flowing through the valley, bringing much-needed water to the flowers.

"I think they're happy now," Violet said.

The ocean spread beneath them in all its beauty.

"I love the ocean," Monica said. "Its color and peace makes me joyful."

"Interesting, when will we at last reach Dragonland?" Violet asked.

"I hope soon," Monica said, but she wasn't sure, because the strange islands that they kept finding made her think that Dragonland was still far.

They started flying through clouds. The clouds

were white and fluffy, and they couldn't see the ocean anymore.

"It's so soft!" Violet exclaimed.

"I have never seen clouds in such a short distance," Monica said. "They're really wonderful."

They flew through them for some time, and then suddenly Monica started sniffing around.

"Violet, the clouds here smell sweet?" Monica said.

"Sweet?" Violet repeated, puzzled.

Monica took a piece of cloud, through which they were passing, and put it into her mouth. It was sweet and very tasty.

"Violet! These are not clouds! These are cotton candies!" Monica exclaimed happily. As she was rather hungry, she started to eat the cotton candies with big pleasure.

"What is a cotton candy, Monica?" Violet asked, sounding surprised.

"It is the tastiest thing in the world, after ice-cream, of course," Monica said. "Eat some and see for yourself."

Her wings flapping, Violet took a small piece of cloud and ate it. Immediately her eyes brightened and she started eating hungrily, without talking.

Monica was laughing: she was glad that Violet had liked the strange clouds that were cotton candies. Even though the cotton candies blocked her view of what was below, Monica managed to notice that the ocean had disappeared.

"There is land below, Violet," Monica exclaimed. "I see land!"

Violet was so busy eating the cotton candies, that she didn't hear Monica.

"Let's get down, Violet!" Monica called, tugging on Violet's ears.

"What are you doing?! Let me eat this tasty stuff!" Violet protested.

"Let's get down: there is land below! Who knows, maybe that's Dragonland!" Monica didn't give up. The last word caught Violet's attention.

"Dragonland? Below?"

"Maybe, who knows?" Monica said, glad that at last Violet was listening.

Violet started descending. They went through fluffy and soft cotton candy until they reached the ground and looked around. The entire ground was covered in cotton candy, but unlike the sky, here the cotton candies were colorful.

"Stop, Monica, don't dismount yet," Violet exclaimed.

"Why?" Monica was surprised.

"I can see strange things here," Violet whispered. "Look!"

Monica looked: in a little distance from them, there were elves and different animals, moving through the cotton candies with difficulty. They didn't look unhappy though. They were eating the delicious sweets happily and talking to one another.

"I think they are stuck here. If you start walking, you may also stick to the sweet candies," Violet said.

"You're such a clever dragon," Monica said in amazement. "You can fly not too high, so we can still be close to them."

Violet started flying near the ground. They passed the different elves and animals.

"What is going on?" Monica asked them. "Why can't you move freely?"

A pretty elf in pink dress looked at them. "This is the Land of Sweet. We got here by mistake, and now can't get out. Not that we want to, anyways, but it would be nicer if we were able to move freely."

"Why is it sticky?" Violet asked.

"Maybe it's magical," another elf joined in the conversation, who was wearing a blue outfit. "But we don't know why."

"Who knows then?"

"There's a Sweet fairy's house not far from here," the first elf said. "And the Sweet fairy lives there in her pretty house. Maybe she knows the answer."

"It's so good that you can fly," the second elf said. "You can directly fly to the Sweet fairy's house without getting stuck."

Monica looked to the direction the elf was pointing. There was a sparkly big house in a distance, glowing in the sunlight.

"Thanks a lot!" She said. "Violet, let's fly to the Sweet fairy's house."

Violet flew towards the glittering house. It seemed to be made of cotton candy, too. Violet flew in through an open window, afraid to land into the sticky cotton candies. The Sweet fairy's house was very beautiful from the inside. It was of different colors and smelled sweetly.

"You can land here, Violet," Monica said.

"No, no," Violet said, trying to fly through the empty hallways of the house. "What if it's sticky here, too? We'll get stuck inside the Sweet fairy's house and will never go to Dragonland!"

Monica giggled. They flew through the hallways and came up to a big door. Violet opened it and flew inside.

A big soft chair was in the middle of the room and a beautiful fairy was sitting on it.

"Welcome to the Land of Sweet," the Sweet fairy said. "But why are you moving? You were supposed to be stuck on my island forever!"

"It's because we're flying," Violet said.

"We have come to ask you why everyone is stuck here," Monica said. "What's happening on your island?"

"It's my little secret," the Sweet fairy said. "But I will tell you because you're not stuck. My island has always been empty. It was a very nice island, with all sorts of sweets and cotton candies, but no one lived here. I was all alone. Whenever traveler elves or animals came to my island, they left. So I decided to make my cotton candies magical and sticky. Now everyone who comes stays here."

Monica and Violet stayed silent. So the cotton candy was magical.

"Dear Sweet fairy," Monica said. "We have talked with the elves today, and they told us that they would gladly stay. You can lift the magic already."

"Will they stay?" The Sweet fairy asked, sounding hopeful.

"Yes, they told us so," Monica said, nodding.

"That's good news!" The Sweet fairy became

happy. "Well, in that case I'll lift the magic, and they will enjoy my island without getting stuck."

"Excellent!" Violet exclaimed.

"And will you stay, too?" The sweet fairy asked them.

"No, we are looking for Dragonland," Monica said. "Violet's parents live there, so we need to go there. Do you know where Dragonland is?"

"Dragonland? Yes, of course," the Sweet fairy said. "But it's a bit far. If you go to the east all the time, you will reach Dragonland. But it's not near here. You still have to go a long way."

"We are ready," Violet said with determination.

"In that case, good luck," the Sweet fairy said.

Monica and Violet waved her goodbye and flew out of the house through the open window.

"Let's eat some more cotton candy as we go," Violet suggested, as they were flying through the sweet candies again.

Monica grabbed handfuls of them and ate with big pleasure. There was ocean below them and soon the cotton candies were replaced with normal clouds again.

Chapter 5. The Many Rainbows

"Do you see land, Monica?" Violet asked after some time.

"Not yet," Monica said. "But if we're going east, that means we shall find land soon."

"The islands that we reached were so interesting," Violet said. "I wonder what other places there are that we shall reach."

"Violet, I think I can see something!" Monica shrieked.

A little ahead of them there was a colorful rainbow sparkling in the sunlight. They descended and saw that it wasn't the only rainbow there: there were many rainbows, crisscrossing one another.

"Rainbows!" Monica exclaimed. "They look like slides! Let's slide down them."

The rainbows were solid and their ends couldn't be seen, because they were descending into a big pit, separated with high and narrow mountaintops.

"But are you sure it's not dangerous?" Violet asked, standing on a rainbow.

"I don't think so," Monica said. She was very excited.

Violet started sliding, Monica on her back.

"Yu-huuu!" Monica shouted. They were sliding down very fast, and the colorful rainbow was spreading in front of them.

"It's so wonderful!" Violet called. She had closed her wings, so that they'd slide down instead of flying.

"This is amazing!" Monica shouted.

Soon they started to slide down the pit where there was no sunshine and it was darker.

"Are you sure we can continue sliding?" Violet asked.

"Yes! Let's go down and see what's on the bottom of the pit," Monica said excitedly.

"But it's so dimly lit," Violet protested.

"Don't worry, we can still see a little," Monica said.

They slid down all the way into the pit and reached the bottom. What they saw caught them by surprise.

There was an entire city on the bottom of the pit. There were people walking in the streets, even though it was semi-dark there.

"Monica, what place is this?" Violet asked. "This surely isn't Dragonland."

"We shall find out soon," Monica said and dismounted.

The people noticed them and came closer to look at them. They were surprised to see Monica and Violet. Soon a crowd of people surrounded them.

"You can fly?" was the first question that they asked Monica and Violet. Then Monica and Violet were flooded with questions.

"What are those wings?"

"How did you get down?"

"Will you help us get out of here?"

Monica and Violet were looking at them. They also had many questions, but the strange inhabitants didn't give them time to ask their questions.

"What is this place called?" Monica asked at last.

"This is Rainbowland," one of the people said. "And there is no way out!"

"What do you mean?" Violet asked, sounding horrified.

"All the rainbows end in this big gap, which is out city," one of them said. "It's impossible to climb up the rainbows, and the walls are so high that it's impossible to climb up the walls, either."

"But why do you live in a gap-city?" Monica asked.

"We used to live in a city which was not in a gap. It was many years ago. There was a rainbow in the sky all the time, that's why our city is called Rainbowland," one girl said. "But then one day suddenly the rainbow multiplied. There were many rainbows instead of one. Just then our city sank into the gap, and since then no one is able to get out."

"Oh, that's really bad," Monica said.

"Our queen is also sad," the girl said. "She lives in that palace, see?"

Monica looked and saw a big palace not far from there. "Violet," she said, mounting her. "Let's go to the queen and ask her how we can help her and these people."

Violet nodded and flew towards the palace. There were guards standing in front of it.

"Who are you and what do you want?" They asked.

"I am Monica and this is Violet, my dragon friend," Monica said hurriedly.

"Actually we weren't even supposed to be here, to tell the truth," Violet interrupted.

"Yes, we were looking for Dragonland, but once we are here, we are interested why your city is in the gap," Monica added.

"So we have come to the queen," Violet added a bit later, seeing that the guards were silent.

The guards looked at each other.

"The thing is," Monica said, "That we may help you. There have been many islands we have visited before, and we have been able to help them, so…"

"All right," one of the guards said, opening the gates.

Monica and Violet entered the palace. It was a beautiful palace, decorated with rainbows.

The queen looked at them in surprise, raising her eyebrows. Before she could say anything, Monica came forward and said:

"Good afternoon. I am Monica and this is Violet, my dragon friend. It's surprising why your city is inside a gap."

"We were flying in the sky, trying to find Dragonland, and we found your island," Violet continued. "It's not a problem for us to fly out of your city, of course, because I have wings and can fly."

"But we are interested in the reason," Monica added.

"It's a very strange story, to tell you the truth," the queen said, sighing. "Something magical happened and the rainbow got damaged – turned into a few rainbows. Our city fell into the gap. If you are able to fly, then you will be able to find the main rainbow and see if you can fix it."

"Fix it?" Monica asked, her eyes sparkling with excitement.

"Yes, fix the rainbow, please. I will be very thankful," the queen repeated.

Monica and Violet looked at each other, their eyes sparkling in anticipation of a new adventure. Violet nodded and Monica mounted. They soared out of the palace and up towards the blue sky. The crowd below gasped and pointed to them, shrieking with amazement.

Chapter 6. Solve It

"This is unbelievable, Violet!" Monica screamed. "I can't believe we're heading for another adventure!"

"I am also excited," Violet said. "But it's a bit scary. How can we find the main rainbow?"

"There is nothing to be afraid of, Violet," Monica said. "We are courageous and kind, that's why we're doing this."

"You are right," Violet said and flew with more determination. There were many rainbows crisscrossing in the sky, and it was a bit confusing.

"How can we know which one is the main one?" Violet asked, looking very confused. She was flipping her wings without going anywhere, looking around. "Maybe we should have asked the queen. She should have known."

"Maybe, but it's too late," Monica said. "Of course we can fly back down and ask her, then return back here, but I think we are clever enough to work it out ourselves."

Violet didn't reply. She was looking around at the numerous colorful rainbows in the sky.

"I, for example, think that we can differentiate them," Monica said.

"How?"

"Well, I think the main one must be bigger, or brighter, or sparkly, something like that. Now let's look for one rainbow that looks a bit different."

Monica and Violet looked around with wide open eyes. All the rainbows seemed the same. Violet started to fly forward slowly, so that they could take a look at all the rainbows.

"I think I have found it!" Violet exclaimed, but then she shook her head, disappointed. "Ah, no, it only seemed to me."

Monica was looking around carefully and concentrating her attention. Suddenly it seemed to her that one of the rainbows glittered differently.

"Violet, let's fly that way," she said, pointing to the rainbow she had noticed.

Violet flew towards that rainbow, even though she hadn't noticed any difference.

"Yes! That's it!" Monica exclaimed.

"What is it?" Violet asked, looking at the rainbow.

"See? It glitters differently," Monica explained. "The sparkles are colorful, and not just silvery."

"Oh, that's right," Violet said, smiling. "Now I can see it, too. But what are we going to do now? We have found it, all right, but what now?"

"I don't know how to fix rainbows, especially when I don't see anything damaged here," Monica said sounding serious.

Violet was flying around the main rainbow, not knowing what to do.

"Look, Violet, how can we know if it's damaged or not, if we are so far from it?" Monica said at last. "Let's get closer and try to stand on it!"

Violet liked the idea. She flew closer and landed right in the center of the rainbow. Monica dismounted. The rainbow was wide enough for both of them to be able to stand on it.

Monica kneeled and started to examine the colorful surface of the rainbow. It was smooth and sparkly. Suddenly she noticed a small hole inside the rainbow. It looked like a keyhole.

"Violet, look! This is a keyhole!" Monica exclaimed.

"So?"

"So, that means that there must be a key somewhere!"

Violet's face brightened as she realized what that meant. "We must look for the key!" with this she flew away, flapping her wings. Monica stayed on the rainbow.

"Violet, take me with you!" She called.

"I think I know where it is!" Violet called from far. She seemed to know where she was flying.

Monica sat down onto the rainbow and hung her feet. She was careful not to slide down the rainbow into the pit-city again. She was already getting worried for Violet when she showed up with the key. It was a small golden key.

"Violet! Where did you get the key from?" Monica asked, her eyes sparkling in amazement.

"I had seen this key in the palace when we were there, Monica," Violet said. "It was in the gates. I asked the guards to give it to me, because it was for fixing the rainbow. They gave it to me silently."

"You're a genius, Violet," Monica said, taking the key and putting it into the hole. It fit. Monica turned the key around a couple of times, and there came a clicking sound. Slowly, as if in a dream, the rainbows started moving.

"Monica, jump onto my back, quickly!" Violet shrieked. Monica jumped onto the dragon's back just in time: the rainbows were moving towards the main rainbow, and they would push Monica off it had she still been standing on it. Soon all the rainbows joined the main one, and it started to sparkle in millions of colors.

Flapping her wings, Violet was standing in the air, looking at the amazing scene. Monica was on her back, holding on tightly. They looked down and saw that the city was coming up. It was moving slowly, and soon Monica and Violet were able to see it fully on the ground. There was no gap anymore.

"The underground city is up!" Violet exclaimed.

The people and the queen of Rainbowland were applauding and greeting Monica and Violet.

"Thank you very much for helping us," the queen said, when they landed on the ground.

"It was a pleasure," the both said together.

"I have a small gift for you," the queen said, giving them a small black box. "Open this when you need help. I think it will help you."

Monica took the box and looked at it, surprised. "Thank you!" She exclaimed. They waved goodbye, as Violet took off again.

Chapter 7. Yet Another Adventure

The ocean was underneath them again. Excited with their ongoing adventures, Monica and Violet were talking nonstop.

"We are so clever, Monica," Violet said, sounding very proud of herself. "We managed to solve the secret of Rainbowland!"

"You are very careful, Violet," Monica said. "If you hadn't noticed the key in the palace gates, we would never be able to unlock the rainbow's magic."

"Thank you, Monica," Violet said. "And you found the main rainbow with the keyhole in it!"

"Yes, that's correct," Monica said. "Hey, I can see land, Violet!" Suddenly she called.

Violet also saw it. It looked like a very tall forest.

Violet started to descend as they reached the land. Monica jumped off and they started to walk. A little bit far from the shore a thick forest was starting. They entered the forest and went forward.

"Monica, look, the trees are so high, and their branches are so intertwined, that I can't see the sky!" Violet said.

"And it seems like sunlight doesn't penetrate here as well," Monica added, as they got deeper into the forest and it became darker.

"Well, Monica, where are we going? Let's fly," Violet said. Monica jumped onto her back, and Violet soared upwards. Unfortunately they found out that the forest had a ceiling made from the tree branches.

"Monica, I can't fly out from the forest!" Violet said, panicking. Monica was also worried.

"All right, let's go back where we came from, and then we shall fly over the forest, not below its ceiling."

Violet turned back and started to fly through the trees, but she didn't remember the way.

"I hadn't flown straight, Monica, and now I don't know where to go," the dragon said.

"Let's try, Violet, after some time we shall come out, don't worry," Monica said, trying to calm Violet down.

Suddenly a gnome appeared from under the trees and squinted, trying to look up at them in the dim light.

"Who are you?" Monica asked. Violet stopped flying.

"I am a gnome, and who are you?"

"I am Monica, and this is my dragon friend, Violet," she said. "It's so good that we found you! Can you tell us the way out of this forest?"

The gnome started laughing. Monica and Violet looked at each other, surprised. When the gnome stopped laughing, he said:

"And I was hoping to find someone who could tell me the way out. Too bad that you don't know either."

"What do you mean?" Monica asked. "What is this place called? Why don't you know the way? Aren't you living here?"

"First of all, this place is called the Island of Labyrinth," the gnome said. "I live here, but not in the forest, no. We – the gnomes – are the inhabitants of the island, but we are forced to enter the forest from time to time to get food. This forest is rich with fruits and berries. A lot of gnomes enter the forest and very few succeed to get out of it."

"What an interesting story!" Violet exclaimed.

"And what an interesting place!" Monica said.

"But when you enter the forest, don't you know that you will get lost?"

"We know," the gnome said.

"Then why don't you take a rope with you and leave a trace behind you, so that you will find the way back without difficulty?" Monica asked.

"This forest has been like this for centuries," the gnome said. "And during all those years everyone has tried to use some kind of a trace, but no one has succeeded. The rope wasn't long enough to take us to the tasty berries, and the corn was quickly eaten by the birds."

"I see," Monica said. "And you haven't even tried to find out why your forest is like this?"

"We have," the gnome said. "Centuries ago the dark witch cast a spell on the forest, and since then it is like this."

"And where is the dark witch now?" Violet asked, looking around fearfully.

"The witch was gone long ago, centuries ago," the gnome said. "But the forest remained like that. Anyways, I hope you will find a way out," the gnome said and walked in another direction.

Monica and Violet shrugged and flew away. Wherever they flew, there was dark forest, and it always seemed to them that the forest was becoming deeper and more intertwined.

"I can't fly anymore," Violet said and landed onto the muddy ground. Monica jumped off and looked around.

"Well, this seems to be a big problem," she said. "Until now we have been able to solve the problems of other islands, and now we can't even solve ours?"

"Yes, we even solved the problems of Rainbowland, which was the most difficult," Violet said.

"Yes, and their queen was very happy for it," Monica said. Suddenly her face brightened. "Violet, the box! The black box! Do you remember that the queen gave us the box and told us to open it whenever we had problems?" she took it out of her pocket.

"Yes," Violet nodded. "And now is the right moment to open it. Go on, open it. I can't wait."

Monica carefully opened the black box. Immediately a blinding white light came out of it and started running through the forest like a bright bird. Wherever the light flew to, that place became filled with light, and soon the entire dark forest was enlightened. The intertwined branches opened up, making the sky visible. The gnomes got out from under the trees and looked around in surprise.

"What is going on?" They were exclaiming.

"Now we can find the way home!"

"This is amazing! I can already see the end of the forest!"

"Look at the sky!"

The gnomes were happy, but the happiest were Monica and Violet, because they had managed to lift the dark magic due to the queen's gift of magical sunray.

Chapter 8. Who Is Violet?

It was late afternoon, and they were flying above the blue ocean. They were tired but happy for their adventures. They were looking forward to reaching Dragonland, though they had no idea how far it was and how many strange islands they were still going to get to. The sun was above the horizon and a warm breeze was playing in the air. Monica was getting worried that her parents would worry about her, but she had to be with her friend, had to help her reach her parents.

The ocean seemed endless.

"Violet, why can't we see land?" Monica asked. "It's been a long time that we're flying, and I can't see anything else besides the ocean."

"Maybe the next island is really far away?" Violet said. Suddenly she noticed that the ocean had a shore, after all. "Monica, does it seem to me, or is there a land over there?"

Monica looked ahead of her attentively. It was an island.

"Fly quickly, Violet!" She called happily. "At last we've found an island! I wonder what adventures await us here."

The land was quickly drawing closer. It was full of mountains, forests and valleys. It seemed to be a very big island.

Violet landed, and Monica jumped off her back, looking around. There was no one there. Suddenly they heard a whooshing sound of wings and saw a big black dragon flying to them.

"Monica, look, a dragon!" Violet said excitedly.

"Yes! I think we are in Dragonland!" Monica clapped her hands.

"At last!"

The dragon came to them and landed. Then its eyes got wider and the dragon shouted:

"I have found the Princess! The Princess is here! Get the King and the Queen as soon as possible!"

While Monica and Violet were looking at each other and shrugging, more dragons arrived, and among them two dragons, which were purple like Violet. They were the king and the queen.

"This is our daughter!" the queen said, coming

towards Violet.

"I am dragon Violet, and this is my best friend Monica from Prettyland. She has helped me to reach Dragonland. But how did I get there?"

"You were in an egg, when the magical winds blew and took you away from Dragonland. We didn't know how to find you, so we hoped that you would find us. And you did!"

"At last I found my land! But I still don't get it: am I a princess?!" Violet asked.

"Yes," all the dragons said together.

Monica and Violet became very happy.

"I'm glad that you found your land and your parents, Violet," Monica said. "But now I have to go home, otherwise my parents will worry. But I don't know how to reach Prettyland."

"Don't worry about it, dear Monica," the queen said. "I know the shortcut to Prettyland. If you enter this small hole in the ground, it will take you to the forest in Prettyland in a very short time. It's a magical hole."

Monica hugged Violet, thanked the queen and entered the hole. Soon she was in the forest, by the hole of the rabbit, and her basket full of flowers was by her side. Smiling with pride and happiness, she ran home. Now that she knew the shortcut to Dragonland, she decided to go and visit Violet often, and even take her friends with her!

- End -

Printed in Great Britain
by Amazon